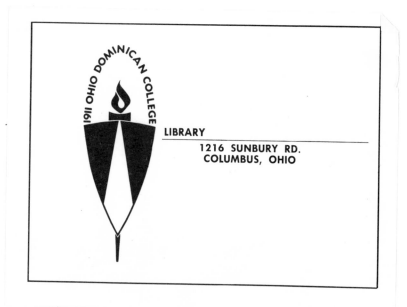

I LOVE MY MOTHER

by

Paul Zindel

pictures by John Melo

HARPER & ROW, PUBLISHERS
New York Evanston San Francisco London

J
Z

To my mother

I love my mother.
She bought me a boa constrictor for my birthday.
I keep it next to my bed.
She taught me how to catch butterflies
and then
let them go.

She showed me how to kick a football.
She has a nice nose and taught me judo.

When I told her I was swallowed by a shark,
she believed it.
But she bought me an aquarium.
I love my mother. I really do.

She gives me piggyback rides in the attic
where the furry creatures fly.

She kisses me before I dream
and turns on the light when the gorilla grabs.

I love my mother.

She let a giraffe eat popcorn off my head at the zoo,
and I threw peanuts to the bears.
She let me ride an elephant, but she came too.

I love my mother.
She makes eggnogs and waffles and cheeseburgers,
and she always saves her last french fry for me.

She says, "Absolutely not,"
when I want to drive the car,

and "Have a good time,"
when I tell her I'm running away to Miami.

She doesn't want me to know
when we don't have enough money.
She thinks I'm going to be a computer programmer.
I'm really going to be a truck driver.

But I'll buy her a diamond ring
and a collie
and a chicken farm
and a thousand flowers.

If I see her crying,
she says, "It's just something in my eye."
She tells me secrets
like she's lonely.

When I tell her I miss my father,
she hugs me
and says
he misses me too.
I love my mother. I really do.

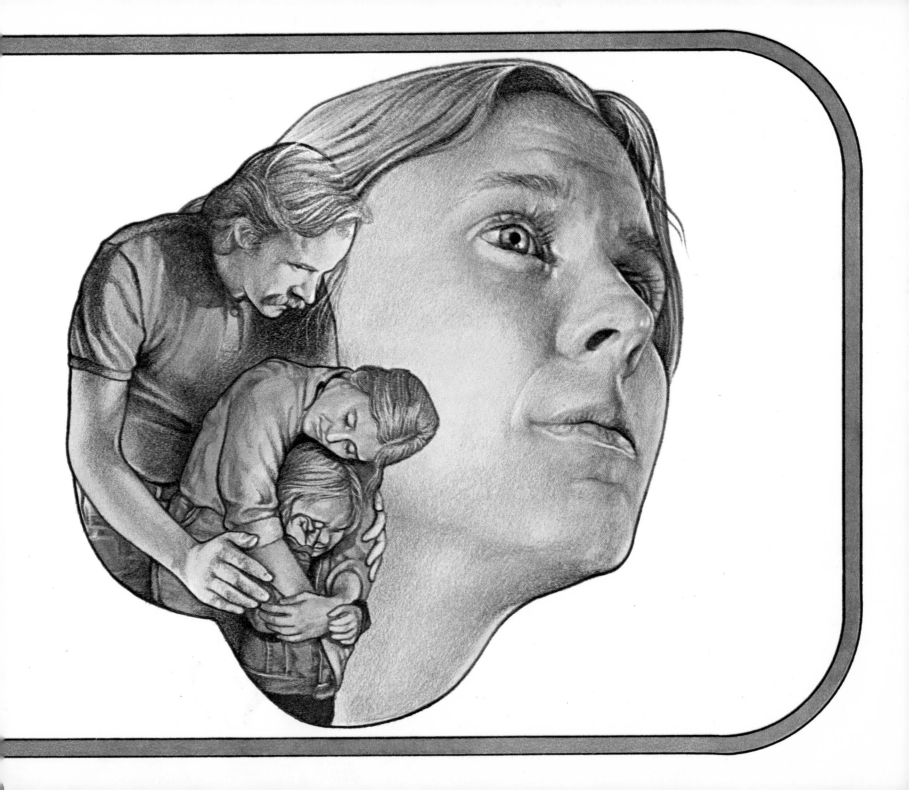

99097

DATE DUE

OCT 18 FACULTY			
FACULTY NOV 18 '78	MAY 07		
MAR 23 '7 FACULTY	AUG 28 1996		
MAY 18 '7 FEB 24 '79	MAY 2 3		
FACULTY APR 05 '79			
JUL 17 7 SEP 26 '79			
FACULTY NOV 29 '79			
OCT 26 '77			
NOV 23 ' MAY 15 '80			
FEB 12 '7 APR. 18 1993			
FACULTY			